DEDICATION

This book is dedicated to my wonderful
and supportive family. My Granddaughter
Genevieve, and my Grandson Bennett.
Also to my wife Suzanne, and my
daughters Chantal, and Kaitlin.

ACKNOWLEDGEMENT

A special thanks to Freisenpress for their
hard work to make this book a reality.

CHAPTER 1

TIBERIUS

Tiberius was a smart, brave, mischievous ten-year-old boy, and he loved adventure. He loved nature and the beauty of the seasons. He loved animals, big and small, and he even had his own pets: pet llamas, pet birds, pet snakes, and many other kinds of exotic animals. He loved the outdoors, loved hunting, loved hiking, swimming, and most of all fishing. He fished for all kinds of fish, but he got tired of that and wanted a bigger adventure.

The break of dawn in the morning was his favourite time, when the bright orange sun broke out of the dark blue sky, and the new day began lighting up the sky with golden rays of sunlight. This is when magic happens, and all dreams can come true.

Tiberius also liked it when the roosters cockled and doodled their melodious, high-pitched sounds that pierced the silent morning air with beautiful music for the soul. This is when you know it's a new day, and adventure is waiting for you.

When Tiberius was born, the village fortune-teller predicted that when he turned fourteen he would become the youngest Village Chief ever, thanks to his bravery, young wisdom, and leadership. He would follow in the footsteps of his grandfather.

CHAPTER 2

THE VILLAGE

Tiberius lived in the little village of Winiperu with his brothers and sisters, and his mom and dad. His brothers and sisters were very young, and he took them to school with him every day. He loved them dearly. Tiberius's father was called Tigron, and his mother's name was Tamala. They were spiritual leaders and also taught in the school. They did missionary work in other villages and were not interested in the village chiefdom. Tiberius was also very close to his grandfather, grandmother, and his uncle.

Tiberius loved school and studied very hard. He excelled in all his subjects. His grandfather also tutored him in survival and leadership skills.

His grandfather's name was Tiberon; he was the Grand Chief of the village, and he gave counsel to the whole village. His grandfather was old and wise and had been a fierce warrior in his day. The village was proud of him.

Tiberius's grandmother, Tarita, was a gifted healer. She used natural herbal medicines from the Amazon rainforest. No one in the village was ever sick, thanks to the love and care she provided.

At school, Tiberius had many friends, but his best friend was Sun-Raya. They were the same age and were both tall and athletic. Sun-Raya was a breath of fresh air and was naturally beautiful like a rainforest pink orchid in bloom.

Tarita taught her natural herbal medicine, and she was also gifted at it.

Like Tiberius, Sun-Raya was good in archery, hand-to-hand combat, and horsemanship.

Winiperu is peaceful and quiet and is nestled in the rainforest of South America, hidden in the Amazon Basin. The village is in a valley. On one side are towering mountain ranges—some jagged, some with long, gentle slopes—and on the other side is a carpet of vibrant green vegetation and rich soil. There is an abundance of graceful waterfalls, many tranquil blue lakes, and rivers with pristine fresh water—as fresh as the early morning dew. The lakes and rivers contain many species of fish, such as payara, bull shark, and catfish. There are hummingbirds, toucans, anteaters, and jaguars.

But the most treasured lake is Lake Winiperu; it gave the fishermen abundant fresh fish every day. This was a bounty for all of the fishermen and for the whole village.

CHAPTER 3
THE MONSTER EEL

Life in this little village was happy and peaceful.

Then, one day, one summer's day, the fishermen ran back to the village and shouted that there were no fish and that there was a Monster Eel that was bigger than a chicken, bigger than a rabbit, bigger than a sheep, bigger than a cow, and bigger than an elephant. It was so big it could swallow up the whole village.

The village elders and all the other villagers ran down to the lake—and it was true that there were no fish. It was also true that there was the Monster Eel. He was slimy, with warts on his back, large black eyes, and sharp, yellow teeth. He was fierce, and he was angry because there were no more fish. He was bigger than a chicken, bigger than a rabbit, bigger than a sheep, bigger than a cow, and bigger than an elephant. He was so big that he could swallow up the whole village.

CHAPTER 4
ARAPAIMA

As the days and weeks passed, food got scarcer and scarcer in the village. The fishermen came home empty-handed every day. People began to grumble and fights broke out. Children cried for food and did not go to school. Tempers flared. It was a scary time.

Tiberius's grandfather, the Grand Chief, held an emergency meeting in the village square. He told the villagers this story: "Many moons ago, my grandfather had the same problem. A Monster Eel had eaten all the fish. My grandfather and his friends trekked for days and days to the lake called Arapaima and brought back the largest and fiercest freshwater fish they could find—the Arapaima fish. In all the Amazon Basin, only Lake Arapaima had the magical, prehistoric Arapaima fish that was as large as a dinosaur. The Arapaima ate the Monster Eel, and the village went back to happy times. It seems as though this happens every hundred years."

The Grand Chief brought out his grandfather's map. It was over one hundred years old, made out of animal skin, and well preserved—but full of dust. He showed the villagers the drawings of the latitude, the North and South bearings, and how to get there. He asked for volunteers to go on the dangerous journey to bring back the Arapaima that was bigger than a chicken, bigger than a rabbit, bigger than a sheep, bigger than a cow, bigger than an elephant, and bigger than the Monster Eel. It could swallow up the Monster Eel and save the whole village.

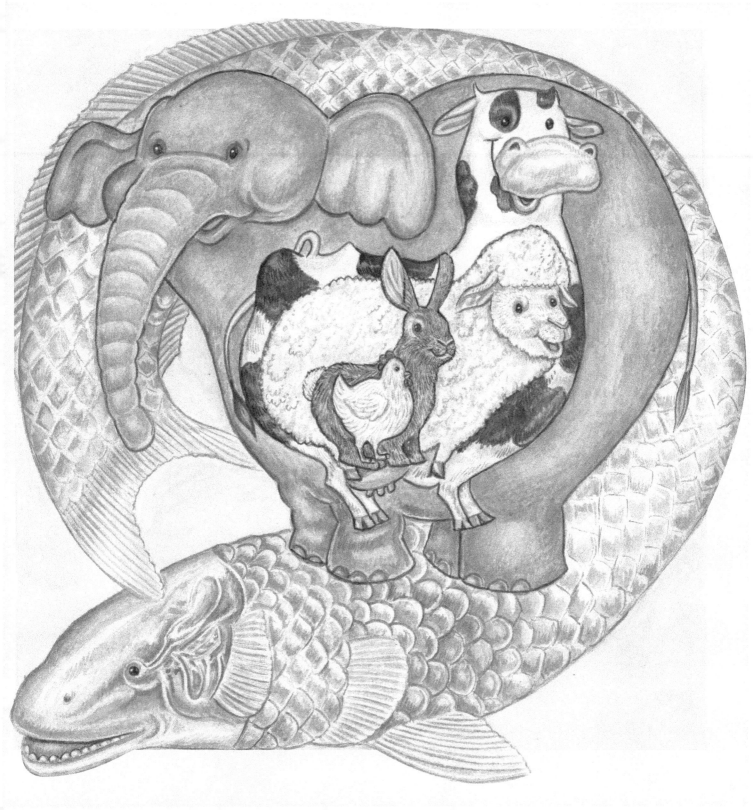

CHAPTER 5
THE PREPARATION

Tiberius and his uncle volunteered along with a few other villagers, including the Blacksmith and the Carpenter. Sun-Raya did not want to be left out of this adventure, so she also volunteered.

Tiberius's uncle was a fierce warrior and loved the outdoors like Tiberius did. He was a good match for any danger to the village and its people.

The volunteers were divided into two teams: the Blacksmith, the Carpenter, and some other villagers were one team. They would build the special wagon that would be bigger than the biggest wagon ever—a wagon big enough to carry a dinosaur.

The other team included Tiberius, his uncle, and Sun-Raya. Their job was to prepare a wagon to transport people. It would be packed with provisions: herbal medicines and food to eat on the journey. They also prepared the fish lines, hooks, and different kinds of fish baits.

The Blacksmith banged here, and he banged there, twisted this, and twisted that. The Carpenter sawed here and sawed there, hammered this, and hammered that. They all worked night and day, and on the third day everything was done.

CHAPTER 6
THE JOURNEY

They started out the next morning before dawn when the whole village was still asleep, even the roosters. The two wagons were fastened up to the horses and filled with everything they needed: herbal medicines, food, clothing, fish bait, and special flints to make fire.

A few miles into the journey, they heard **clang**, **clang**, **clang** coming from the bottom of the Arapaima wagon. Something was broken. The convoy stopped, and Tiberius jumped down. It was still dark, so Tiberius took the lantern and started checking, and to his dismay, he saw that one of the wheels was broken!

So they had to turn back, back to the village with a **clang**, **clang**, **clang**.

They went straight to the Blacksmith's house and told him the problem. The Blacksmith lived close to his shop and hurried over in his pajamas. The Blacksmith banged here, and he banged there, and after a few hours, he was finished—all of the wheels were now round.

They left the village at a much later time, and there was no more **clang**, **clang**, **clang**. The journey was smooth, and they travelled until nightfall and then set up camp. They lit a large fire, ate some food, and slept fitfully.

Tiberius stood guard for the first half of the night, and his uncle stood guard for the second half of the night. It was dark and cold. They were the bravest warriors in the village and had no fear. During Tiberius's watch, a large, angry black bear approached their tent with a wild roar and was about to attack. But Tiberius, being a brave warrior, was calm and just

banged two large stones together. The noise caused the bear to scamper away. Tiberius had his bow and arrow ready, but he did not want to kill the bear.

During Tiberius's watch another incident occurred. An old jaguar was circling the tent in search of food—he was hungry, and his mouth was watering. When he smelled the meat and the fish, he became furious. He growled fiercely and approached Tiberius. Tiberius had nerves of steel and did not flinch. He was fast on his feet and grabbed a flaming log from the fire. He advanced towards the jaguar, waving the flames with a **whoosh** and a **swoosh**, and a **whoosh** and a **swoosh**, and the jaguar scooted away on his big paws.

The next morning, they continued the journey and arrived at Lake Arapaima as dusk fell. They camped for the night—exhausted, but happy and relieved after missing the trail a few times and the scary animal attacks.

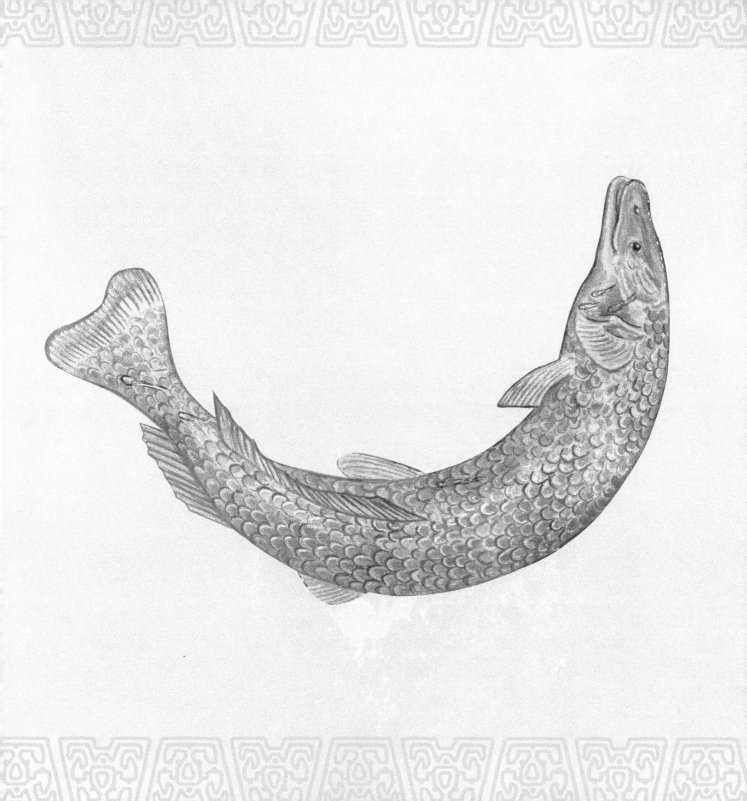

CHAPTER 7

THE BIG CATCH

The next morning, they began the preparation. They spread out the fishing line on the sand beside the lake, attached the hook, and attached the bait, which was beef. They threw the line in with a big **splash**. They waited and they waited. There was no tug on the line, so they pulled it in, and there was no bait and no fish. The Arapaima had outsmarted them.

Now, a second time, they baited their hook with new, fresh bait, which was fish, and threw their line out further, with two big splashes—**Splash, Splash**. They waited, and waited, and they waited. They could not wait any longer, and gingerly, they pulled the line in. There was no bait, and no fish. The Arapaima had outsmarted them again.

Now Tiberius, being a smart kid and knowing the habits of fish, thought of a different approach. "Uncle, why don't we try a corn cob as bait?" His uncle was a bit taken aback. This had never been done before. "Okay nephew, we will try a corn cob. It can't hurt."

They attached the corn cob to the hook and threw the line out as far as they could, now with three big splashes—SPLASH, SPLASH, SPLASH.

They waited, and waited, and waited. Suddenly, the line shook and then tugged. The Arapaima jumped in the air, pulling here, and pulling there, and everywhere. Then they all grabbed the fish line—Tiberius, his uncle, and the other village folks. They pulled and pulled on the line to bring in the Arapaima. The fish line stretched, it became taut, and with a loud snap, it broke.

This all happened next to the shoreline, and now the Arapaima was attempting to swim away. But Tiberius and Sun-Raya were both fast on their feet. They grabbed the large fish net they had made especially for this occasion. One was on the left side of the net, and one was on the right side. They ran into the water up to their knees, and, with all of their strength, they threw the net over the Arapaima.

The Arapaima was now securely in the net. There was a large sigh of relief from all the villagers. As fast as they could, they all pulled the wiggling fish onto the land and put him into the special wagon filled with fresh lake water to keep him alive and safe. They fed him some food, and Sun-Raya put some herbal medicine on a little bruise on his fin. The Arapaima was now safe for the home journey.

CHAPTER 8
THE RETURN HOME

They began the journey back home immediately, as they did not want to waste time.

It was dark, and they had travelled a good distance, and they were getting tired with the lack of sleep, and so they did not pay attention to the map. They drifted off onto the wrong path. It was raining dreadfully, and it was very slippery.

Suddenly, the wagon carrying some of the village folk and the provisions stopped in its path and could not move. Tiberius and Sun-Raya were in this wagon; Tiberius's uncle was in the second wagon, carrying the Arapaima, way far behind. Tiberius took the lantern and shone it, and realized his wagon was stuck in quicksand and would soon begin to sink, along with the village folks and the horse.

The horse was neighing with panic because it was beginning to get sucked into the quicksand.

Tiberius leaped into action, and the first thing he did was to signal his uncle to stop and not go any further.

The rain was blinding him, and he wiped his eyes in order to see properly.

The next thing he did was jump off the wagon—to the side, to avoid the quicksand—and attach separate ropes to the horse and the wagon. He tied the other ends of the ropes to some large trees for support. This was to ensure that the horse and the wagon did not sink any further into the quicksand. The others watched what he was doing and quickly caught

on. They threw some large stones into the quicksand to build a foundation, and then they cut some trees. They put the tree trunks on top of the rocks and attached them together with vines to make a platform, so that the horse could have something solid to step onto. Next, they all pulled the horse to safety.

Now, they attached the ropes to the horse and to the wagon. With all the manpower and the horsepower, they pulled the wagon free. There was a stream nearby, and they washed the horse and the wagon.

After a little rest, they resumed their journey back home. They were more careful this time.

CHAPTER 9
THE ARRIVAL

Tiberius, Sun-Raya, and the other villagers arrived back home to a hero's welcome. All of the village folks—including Tiberius's grandfather, his grandmother, his mom and dad, and his brother and sisters—were there to meet them. Everyone was there, even the Blacksmith and the Carpenter.

Wasting no time, they all slid the Arapaima into Lake Winiperu with a big **splash**. The Arapaima bubbled up and down, swimming here and there as happy as can be. This was a fresher and cleaner lake than Lake Arapaima. The Arapaima was bigger than a chicken, bigger than a rabbit, bigger than a

sheep, bigger than a cow, bigger than an elephant, and bigger than the Monster Eel. It swallowed up the Monster Eel with one mighty gulp and saved the whole village.

The other fish came back in abundance—healthier and tastier. There were so many fish that the children could reach into the lake and play with them. The Arapaima and the villagers shared the Lake Winiperu fish.

The whole village was happier and more peaceful, and everything went back to normal.

CHAPTER 10

RETURN TO LAKE ARAPAIMA

Tiberius and his uncle planned to return to Lake Arapaima and bring back a companion for their Arapaima friend, because he was lonely. And guess who refused to be left out of this next adventure? Sun-Raya. She enjoyed adventures so much, so she became part of the team.

This time, they waited for the fortune-teller to tell them when the next equinox would be. The fortune-teller predicted, "On the next equinox, the night will have a full moon for three days, and it will be bright as day, and it will be a good time to travel."

They prepared the two wagons for the return journey to Lake Arapaima: one for provisions and some villagers, and the other to bring back another Arapaima for company. They knew exactly what to take—especially the one-hundred-year-old leather map.

With all the preparation, the experience they'd gained from the previous journey, and the advice of the fortune-teller, they travelled to Lake Arapaima and back without a hitch. They brought back another Arapaima and put it in the lake, and everything was beautiful.

CHAPTER 11

A PARTY FOR HEROES

With everything back to normal, Tiberius's grandfather, the Grand Chief, declared a holiday in the village. It was to be called "Arapaima Holiday".

There was a whole week of celebrations, with lots of food and drink, and lots of music and dancing. Many musicians, acrobats, and dancers came from the surrounding villages. There was happiness all over. On the last day of the festivities, Tiberius's grandfather said to the cheering crowd, over the noise, "Today I decree that as soon as Tiberius is fourteen years old, he will become the next Grand Chief, and I will retire."

Grand Chief Tiberon told all the village folks to start preparations for their new Grand Chief.

CHAPTER 12
GRAND CHIEF TIBERIUS

Four years later ...

And so it came to pass that at just fourteen years of age, Tiberius became the youngest Grand Chief in all of the villages of the Amazon Basin. Sun-Raya became a great medicine woman in her own right. Tiberius often sought her advice.

This was the biggest celebration there had been in the Amazon Basin for hundreds of years. This was bigger than the party for heroes. The celebration lasted for one month, to allow all the

Village Grand Chiefs to attend, because many of them came from far away. They brought lots of gifts—including gold, herbs, spices, swords, and bows and arrows.

Every day of the celebration, the Grand Chiefs smoked their peace pipes to focus on peace and friendship in the villages. Tiberius's mother and father, as well as the other spiritual leaders, blessed everything and everyone—and Tiberius, most of all.

There were parades up and down the streets in ceremonial gear and with trumpets, horns, and drums, which filled the air with music for the soul. People danced the night away. To end the night, there were colourful fireworks.

On the last day of the celebrations, fourteen doves of peace were released, representing Tiberius's tender age.

CHAPTER 13

THE END

Tiberius was fair and honest in every decision he made as Chief. All the other Grand Chiefs from all the other villages came for counsel from Sun-Raya and Tiberius.

With Tiberius's guidance, Winiperu became the most prosperous village in all of the rainforest. Trade in fish, gold, herbs, and spices flourished. All the other villages wanted to buy from Winiperu.

As Tiberius grew older, with more wisdom and experience, he would often speak to the young ones. He would say, "You have to study hard and listen to your teachers, parents, and grandparents. Do not give up on your dreams. Life is an adventure every day, and the universe gives you opportunities. Listen to your heart and soul, and go for what you want with desire and passion. Finally, love what you do—dreams do come true."

And everyone lived happily in Village Winiperu. Long Live Tiberius, the best Grand Chief ever!

THE END

ABOUT THE AUTHOR

Like Tiberius, Patrick V. London spent a happy and adventurous childhood in a village in the Amazonian Basin in South America. At 10 years old, he too witnessed the catch of a mighty Arapaima—the largest freshwater fish in the Amazon rainforest—by his uncle and other villagers.

London is a father and grandfather, and lives in Oshawa, Ontario with his wife, Suzanne. The birth of twin grandchildren inspired Tiberius's story.

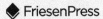

◆ FriesenPress

Suite 300 - 990 Fort St
Victoria, BC, V8V 3K2
Canada

www.friesenpress.com

Tiberius, Arapaima, and the Monster Eel, is a story about a brave, mischievous 10 year old boy and his adventure with his best friend, and his uncle into the vast Amazon rainforest to catch the biggest fish to save his village. He becomes a hero, and in the end becomes the youngest Grand Chief at 14 years old in the Amazon Basin. His advice to the kids is to listen to your parents, listen to your heart and soul. Don't give up, love what you do. Dreams do come true.

ISBN
978-1-5255-5466-7 (Hardcover)
978-1-5255-5467-4 (Paperback)
978-1-5255-5468-1 (eBook)

1. JUVENILE FICTION

Distributed to the trade by The Ingram Book Company

Lightning Source UK Ltd.
Milton Keynes UK
UKHW050321170620
364916UK00007B/64